Aztec Beliefs

Carmel Reilly

NELSON
CENGAGE Learning™

Australia • Brazil • Japan • Korea • Mexico • Singapore • Spain • United Kingdom • United States

Aztec Beliefs

Fast Forward
Silver Level 23

Text: Carmel Reilly
Editor: Johanna Rohan
Design: Stella Vassiliou
Series design: James Lowe
Production controller: Seona Galbally
Photo research: Gillian Cardinal
Audio recordings: Juliet Hill, Picture Start
Spoken by: Matthew King and Abbe Holmes
Reprint: Jennifer Foo

Acknowledgements
The author and publisher would like to acknowledge permission to reproduce material from the following sources:

Photographs by
Front cover: The Art Archive/Museo Ciudad Mexico/Dagli Orti
Back cover: The Art Archive/National Anthropological Museum Mexico/Dagli Orti
The Art Archive/Museo Ciudad Mexico/Dagli Orti, pp 1, 4-5, 8 -9, 10 right, 12, 23/ Mexican National Library/ Mireille Vautier, p 10 left/ National Anthropological Museum Mexico/Dagli Orti, p 10 right, 14-15, 20/ Biblioteca Nacional Madrid/Dagli Orti, p 11/ Templo Mayor Library/Dagi Orti, p 16/ Bodleian Library, p 19/ Museo Franz Mayer/Dagli Orti, p 22; Corbis Australia Pty Ltd, pp 7, 13; Photolibrary, pp 6, 17-18, 21.

ISBN 978 0 17 012699 1
ISBN 978 0 17 012693 9 (set)

Cengage Learning Australia
Level 7, 80 Dorcas Street
South Melbourne, Victoria Australia 3205
Phone: 1300 790 853

Cengage Learning New Zealand
Unit 4B Rosedale Office Park
331 Rosedale Road, Albany, North Shore NZ 0632
Phone: 0800 449 725

For learning solutions, visit **cengage.com.au**

Printed in Australia by Ligare Pty Ltd
6 7 8 9 10 11 12 21 20 19 18 17

THE UNIVERSITY OF MELBOURNE

Evaluated in independent research by staff from the Department of Language, Literacy and Arts Education at the University of Melbourne.

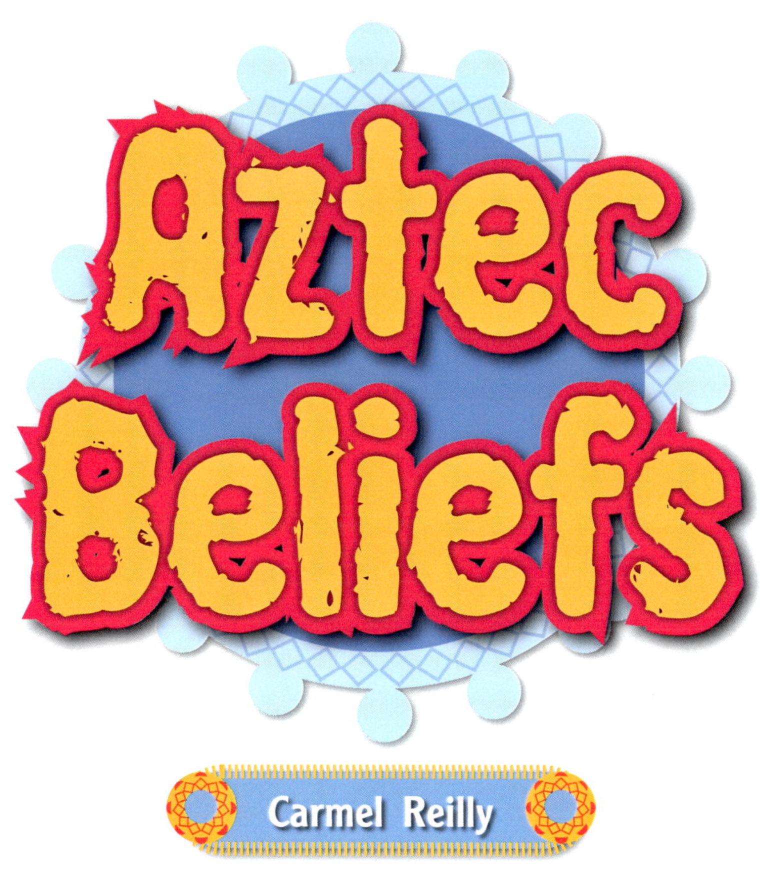

Aztec Beliefs

Carmel Reilly

Contents

Chapter 1

THE AZTECS

The Aztecs were a native American people who lived in **Central America** between the 14th and 16th centuries. The Aztecs were originally from North America, but they migrated south to the area that is now modern Mexico in search of a better place to live.

two Toltec people

When the Aztecs first arrived in Central America,
they were subjects of the **Toltec** people
who already ruled the area.
But, when the Aztecs had been there for about 100 years,
they started to set up their own empire.
Over the next 100 years,
this empire grew to cover the area
that is now Mexico and Guatemala.

Chapter 2

AZTEC SOCIETY

A Culture of Classes

The Aztec population was divided into four main classes. **Nobles** were the highest and most powerful class. They included the emperor and his extended family, as well as governors in charge of local areas, and members of the government. The nobles owned most of the land.

Montezuma, an Aztec ruler, and his governors

an Aztec man harvesting corn

Commoners made up most of the population.
They ran small family farms
or did ordinary jobs in the towns and cities.

Serfs worked on the land owned by the nobles.
They were given food and shelter, but weren't paid.

Slaves were either prisoners of war
or criminals who could be bought and sold.

The City

Many Aztec people lived in rural villages, working the land.
However, many more lived in large towns and cities.
Tenochtitlan, the Aztec capital and home to the emperor, became one of the largest cities in the world.
Its construction began in 1325 AD, and it's believed that by 1500 AD more than 200000 people lived there.

the Aztec capital, Tenochtitlan

the Great Temple in the centre of Tenochtitlan

As with all Aztec towns and cities, there was a central area for temples and other special places in Tenochtitlan. People could gather there to worship the Aztec gods.

Chapter 3

AZTEC RELIGIOUS BELIEFS

The Gods

Religion was important to all Aztec people, and they worshipped hundreds of different gods. Many of these gods represented farming, the natural elements and the seasons. They included a corn god, a sun god, a fire god, a wind god, a god of spring and a god of the dead.

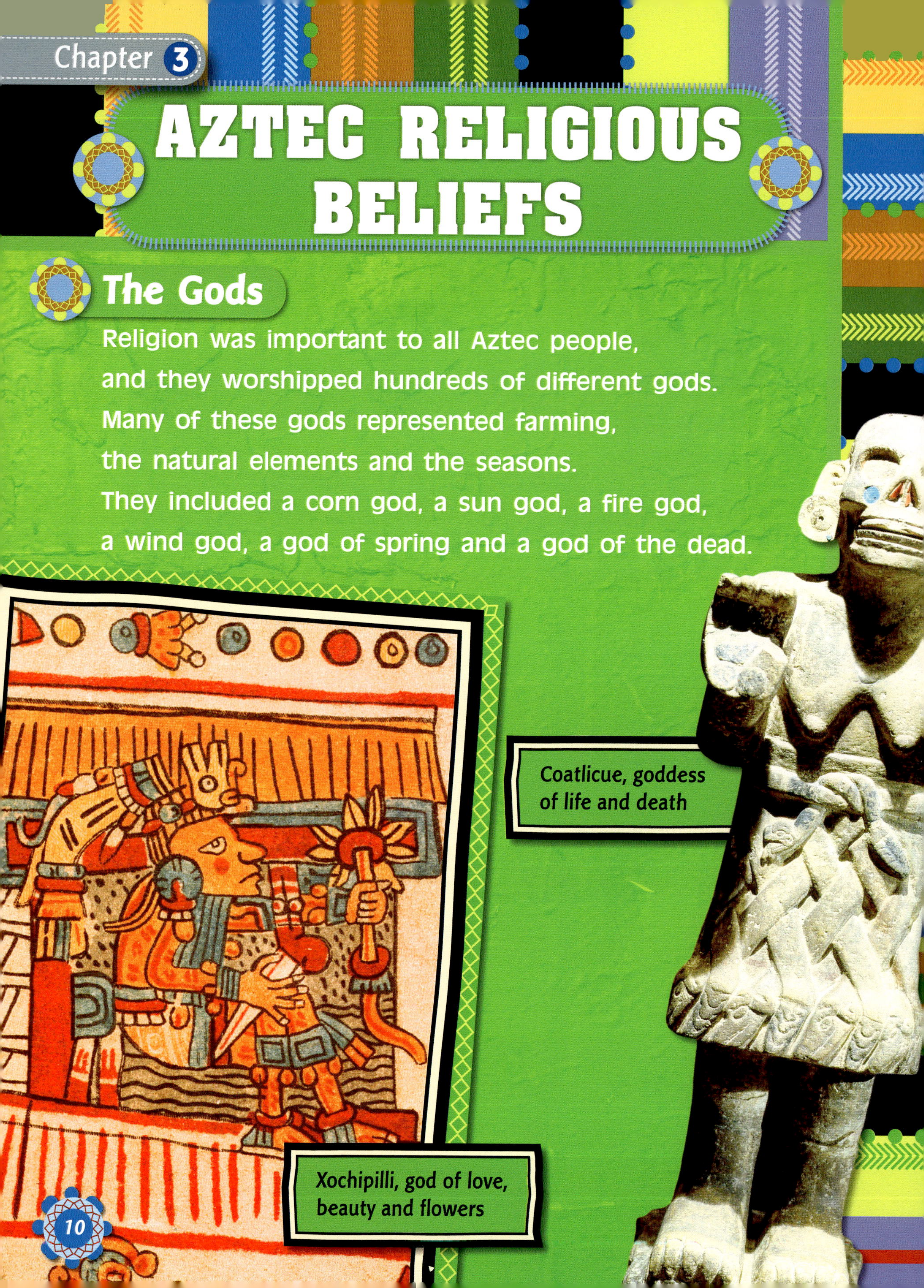

Coatlicue, goddess of life and death

Xochipilli, god of love, beauty and flowers

an Aztec ceremony

The Aztecs held many religious ceremonies
that were a part of the farming cycle
of planting and harvesting.
In these ceremonies, they called on the gods
to protect them and give them good crops
so that there would be enough food for everyone
throughout the year.

Festivals

A big part of Aztec life was festivals to honour and thank the gods. The festivals usually took place in special areas that had been created near the temples in the centre of towns and cities. These areas were big enough for large crowds to gather to eat, drink, sing, dance and worship.

a large crowd gathers at the Great Temple, in Tenochtitlan

Aztec musicians

Music and entertainment were a big part
of these festivals.
Aztec orchestras were common,
with people using large shells, played like trumpets,
and flutes, rattles, drums and whistles.

Offerings

Aztec people made all kinds of offerings to their gods. Most Aztec people pricked their ears each morning and collected two drops of blood to offer up to the gods.

There were also other more everyday offerings to the gods of fruit, vegetables and flowers. These offerings were left at the steps of the temples. The Aztecs believed that the more valuable the gift, the more it would please the gods.

Sacrifices

Sacrifices were a big part of the Aztec religion, and many of their larger festivals included human offerings.

Like the **Mayan** and the Toltec people before them, the Aztecs believed that the world would end unless they made offerings of blood and human lives to the gods.

an Aztec human sacrifice

an Aztec human sacrifice

Most human sacrifices were of prisoners of war. Sometimes, only one or two people would be offered up to the gods at a festival.

At other times, such as when the Great Temple in the centre of Tenochtitlan was finished in 1487, thousands of prisoners were sacrificed at once.

Warfare

Warfare was important to the Aztecs because they wanted to protect their empire and extend their territory and trade. Warfare was also important to the Aztecs because it meant they could take prisoners to use as slaves and sacrifices to the gods.

Aztec warriors in battle

Aztec warriors

Warfare was seen as a part of Aztec religious duty. The highest goal for a man was to be a good warrior. Soldiers were admired because they took prisoners and because of their bravery, **honour** and physical fitness. The Aztec people believed these qualities were the most important qualities a man could have.

Chapter 4

FEARS FOR THE FUTURE

The Aztecs offered prayers, gifts and sacrifices
to the gods so that they would look kindly on them.
The Aztec people were always afraid
that their gods would turn against them
and that the world would end.
Aztec legends said that the world had ended
a number of times before,
but it had been born again.
However, the legends also said that the next time
the world ended would be the last time.

Montezuma, an Aztec ruler, watching the 1519 comet

It was believed that there would be many heavenly signs to let the people know that the end of the world was coming.
These signs included comets and solar and lunar eclipses.
In 1517, these signs began to come.

The End of the Aztec World

In 1519, a large comet with a fiery tail appeared in the sky over Aztec lands. There was also a solar eclipse at about the same time. Soon after, the Aztec empire was invaded by the Spanish. Although the Spanish didn't have many soldiers, they had horses, wagons and guns. Within two years, they had defeated the Aztecs and taken over most of their lands.

fighting between the Aztecs and the Spanish

Although the world didn't come to an end, the Aztec empire did.
By 1521, the Spanish had destroyed the great capital of Tenochtitlan and had begun building Mexico City on its site.
Spanish settlers began moving to Central America, bringing a new culture and set of religious beliefs that would take over from those of the Aztecs.

Spanish settlers building Mexico City on the Tenochtitlan site

Glossary

Central America the narrow part of land between North America and South America

Mayan native people of Central America

honour a feeling of pride

nobles people belonging, by title, rank or birth, to the upper social group

sacrifices rituals involving killing humans or animals as an offering to the gods

serfs people forced to work on the land

Toltec native people of Central America, before the Aztecs

Index